3/17/21

~~NOV 1 9 2020~~

D1156174

RHODA
THE ALLIGATOR

by Governor Bob Graham

illustrated by Jay Winter Collins

Rhoda was born on a
tree island in the Florida
Everglades.

Most of the Everglades is slow-moving water—home to a unique mix of plants, animals, birds, fish, and reptiles that can't be found anywhere else on Earth.

Rhoda, bright, colorful, and full of life, lived in a swampy bog with her mother, father, and older brother Felix.

Summers in the Glades are wet,
the pouring rains providing the water needed
to support the beautiful variety of life.

From the tiny mosquito to the mighty panther,
all creatures live in harmony and balance,
supporting each other and their
unique Everglades home.

As Rhoda swam through the Glades,
she saw other bay alligators,
but they did not look like her.

The other baby alligators were the colors
of the Everglades.
But not Rhoda, Rhoda was different.

One day, Rhoda's mother took her to the baby pool,
where the other baby alligators played.
Horace, the biggest of the baby alligators,
swam towards Rhoda.

Was he about to ask her to be his friend?
But that was not the case.
Horace bumped Rhoda and said, "You look weird.
Not like any alligator I've ever seen.
You can't be my friend.
Your colors are all wrong. Please leave."

Rhoda felt mad and sad.
Her eyes filled with tears
as she yelled at Horace,
"Well, you are not perfect either!
Your teeth are crooked,
and your nose is too spotty."

Rhoda ran to her safe place on her mother's head.
"What did he mean when he said I don't look like
a real alligator?" Rhoda asked her mother.
So Rhoda's mother sank below the water
with Rhoda so that she could see herself
reflected above.

"Mother, I don't want to be different.
I just want to fit in and make friends."

"Look all around you, Rhoda," her mother said.
"Like you, the Everglades is special.
There is no place like it in the world.
The water, the sawgrass, the sun, the rain,
and the trees are all different from each other,
yet they all add something to this beautiful place."

Rhoda thought about what her mother said.
How it is our differences that make us special.
But like the sun and the rains learned to accept
their differences and work together, so would
Rhoda if she was to help keep the balance
of the Everglades.

The next day, after the thunderstorm passed and the sun came out, Rhoda went searching for Horace. "I am sorry for what I said about your nose and teeth," she said. "I learned that we should not treat each other badly because we look different. It is the differences that make the Everglades a unique place and each of us unique alligators."

"I'm sorry too, Rhoda," said Horace.
"I like your bright colors."

Rhoda flapped her tail. "Being different can be scary. But without our differences our world, and especially our Everglades home, would not be as interesting... or as much fun."

They both agreed that there was no place on Earth where being different was more okay than the Florida Everglades.

Using her new understanding of acceptance
and compassion, Rhoda went off to explore
the nearby waterways of the Glades,
in the hope of making new friends and helping
all of its wonderful creatures feel accepted
and live in balance and harmony.

The End

Cover Design: Morgane Leoni
Illustrations: Jay Winter Collins
Layout & Design: Morgane Leoni & Kim Balacuit
With editorial guidance and help from Margaret Cardillo

For permission requests, please contact the publisher at:
Mango Publishing Group
2850 S Douglas Road, 2nd Floor
Coral Gables, FL 33134 USA
info@mango.bz

For special orders, quantity sales, course adoptions and corporate sales, please email the publisher at sales@mango.bz. For trade and wholesale sales, please contact Ingram Publisher Services at customer.service@ingramcontent.com or +1.800.509.4887.

Rhoda the Alligator: A Children's Book about Acceptance

Library of Congress Cataloging-in-Publication number: 2020940956
ISBN: (print) 978-1-63353-954-9, (ebook) 978-1-63353-955-6
BISAC category code JUV039230, JUVENILE FICTION / Social Themes / Bullying

Printed in the United States of America

Acknowledgements

Of the names I've had in my life, my favorite is "Doodle," which is what my eleven grandchildren call me. I have been telling Rhoda's story to my grandchildren and their cousins and friends for ten years now. With the encouragement of my granddaughters, Caroline Adele McCullough and Melissa Gwendolyn McCullough, and my adopted granddaughter, Louisa Ahl McCullough, we decided it would be fun to turn my Rhoda nighttime story into a children's book. The time the four of us spent together working on *Rhoda the Alligator* was so very special, and I could not have captured Rhoda's childlike joy without their help and love. I hope all children and the grownups in their lives who read *Rhoda the Alligator* together will experience the same joy.

About the Author

When you consider the profound sweep of his life, public service, and the stature he's earned, Daniel Robert "Bob" Graham is not the first person you might expect to author a book for children of all ages and their families. Bob is a lifelong Democrat, Harvard Law School alumni, and was a Member of the Florida House of Representatives and the Florida State Senate. His legacy of dedicated service continues today through his work at The Bob Graham Center for Public Service, located at his alma mater, The University of Florida.

Telling his family stories and teaching his children and grandchildren life lessons, like those found in Rhoda, has always been most important to him and his loving wife, Adele.

Afterword

For the children in my own wonderful family, Rhoda's story is very familiar. I've been telling it to them for years.

It's a tale meant to empower the listener, and now the reader, with a simple-yet-forceful message: embrace the unique qualities and exceptional gifts each of us has to offer the world.

In writing this book, I sought to carry that message forward to children and to people of all ages—whom I could not reach as a father and grandfather. I hope you enjoy the story, the time spent sharing it with your children, and the inspiration both you and they may draw from Rhoda. Those precious moments and memories with our own children and grandchildren are the times Adele and I cherish most.

Rhoda the Alligator's setting is also important, meant to highlight and celebrate the Florida Everglades, just one unique treasure among many in the US National Park System.

If you've never seen the Everglades, I implore you to imagine it as more than a "swamp" (that word implies a murky, worthless tract of land). Conservationist Marjory Stoneman Douglas painted a glorious picture of the Everglades as a "vast glittering openness." In her seminal work of the same name, she also profoundly redefined the Everglades as a "river of grass." This one-of-a kind region is exactly that: a river of slow-moving water that flows south from Lake Okeechobee.

At 1.5 million acres, the Everglades is now less than half its original size due to construction and drainage projects over the years that overlooked the value and vitality of the wetlands. Despite its diminished size, the Everglades provides water to eight million Floridians, and is the third largest US National Park—right behind Yellowstone and Death Valley. The wetlands preserve—brought into the National Park System in 1947—consists of nine distinct ecosystems that are habitat and home to many animals like Rhoda, and more—with at least 750 fish, bird, mammal, and reptile species. These include endangered species like the Florida panther and American crocodile.

Created in 1916, the park system's mission is to maintain and protect the ecological and historical integrity of America's natural resources. By preserving important regions and making them accessible to the public, the NPS helps and encourages Americans to maintain a connection to some of the country's irreplaceable gifts of nature. Visitors who take a day trip out to the Everglades can see the home of our indigenous forbearers and also, as President Harry S. Truman concluded when dedicating the park, commune with nature as a way of enriching their spirits.

As with other jewels of the park system, the Everglades have been important to my family for years. While its current status as a National Park offers it some protections, we must do more to maintain, and restore, our precious wetlands. One thing you can do is go online and learn more. The Friends of the Everglades (everglades.org), an organization established by Marjory Stoneman Douglas in 1969, is a great place for children and their parents to learn more about the Everglades and how to get involved. I hope that, like me, you fall in love with the uniqueness of the Everglades and work to keep it around for your kids, their kids, and beautiful animals like Rhoda.

I'm humbled to witness something as breathtaking and awe-inspiring as our Florida Everglades. Just as I am humbled that you might read Rhoda's story and share its message with the next generations of your own family.

-Bob Graham

Mango Publishing, established in 2014, publishes an eclectic list of books by diverse authors—both new and established voices—on topics ranging from business, personal growth, women's empowerment, LGBTQ studies, health, and spirituality to history, popular culture, time management, decluttering, lifestyle, mental wellness, aging, and sustainable living. We were recently named 2019 and 2020's #1 fastest growing independent publisher by Publishers Weekly. Our success is driven by our main goal, which is to publish high quality books that will entertain readers as well as make a positive difference in their lives.

Our readers are our most important resource; we value your input, suggestions, and ideas. We'd love to hear from you—after all, we are publishing books for you!

Please stay in touch with us and follow us at:
Facebook: Mango Publishing
Twitter: @MangoPublishing
Instagram: @MangoPublishing
LinkedIn: Mango Publishing
Pinterest: Mango Publishing

Newsletter: mangopublishinggroup.com/newsletter
Join us on Mango's journey to reinvent publishing, one book at a time.